I0452453

THE FIRE OF ASSHURBANIPAL

BY

ROBERT E. HOWARD

Copyright © 2013 Read Books Ltd.
This book is copyright and may not be
reproduced or copied in any way without
the express permission of the publisher in writing

British Library Cataloguing-in-Publication Data
A catalogue record for this book is available from the
British Library

Robert E. Howard

Robert Ervin Howard was born in Peaster, Texas in 1906. During his youth, his family moved between a variety of Texan boomtowns, and Howard – a bookish and somewhat introverted child – was steeped in the violent myths and legends of the Old South. Although he loved reading and learning, Howard developed a distinctly Texan, hardboiled outlook on the world. He became a passionate fan of boxing, taking it up at an amateur level, and from the age of nine began to write adventure tales of semi-historical bloodshed. In 1919, when Howard was thirteen, his family moved to the Central Texas hamlet of Cross Plains, where he would stay for the rest of his life.

At fifteen Howard began to read the pulp magazines of the day, and to write more seriously. The December 1922 issue of his high school newspaper featured two of his stories, 'Golden Hope Christmas' and 'West is West'. In 1924 he sold his first piece – a short caveman tale titled 'Spear and Fang' – for $16 to the not-yet-famous *Weird Tales* magazine. He published with the magazine regularly over the next few years. 1929 was a breakout year for Howard, in that the 23-year-old writer began to sell to other magazines, such as *Ghost Stories* and *Argosy*, both of whom had previously sent him hundreds of rejection slips. In 1930, he began a correspondence with weird fiction master H. P. Lovecraft which ran up to his death six years later, and is regarded as one of the great correspondence cycles in all of fantasy literature.

It was partly due to Lovecraft's encouragement that Howard created his most famous character, Conan the Cimmerian. Conan – a barbarian-turned-King during the Hyborian Age, a mythical period of some 12,000 years ago – featured in seventeen *Weird Tales* stories between 1933 and 1936, and is now regarded as having spawned the 'sword and sorcery' genre, making Howard's influence on fantasy literature comparable to that of J. R. R. Tolkien's. The Conan stories have since been adapted many times, most famously in the series of films starring Arnold Schwarzenegger.

Howard was enjoying an all-time high in sales by the beginning of 1936, but he was also deeply upset by the ill health of his mother, who had fallen into a coma. On the morning of June 11, 1936, he asked an attending nurse whether she would ever recover, and the nurse replied negatively. Howard walked to his car, parked outside the family home in Cross Plains, and shot himself. He died eight hours later, aged just thirty.

YAR Am squinted carefully down the blue barrel of his Lee-Enfield, called devoutly on Allah and sent a bullet through the brain of a flying rider.

"Allaho akbar!"

The big Afghan shouted in glee, waving his weapon above his head, "God is great! By Allah, sahib, I have sent another one of the dogs to Hell!"

His companion peered cautiously over the rim of the sand-pit they had scooped with their hands. He was a lean and wiry American, Steve Clarney by name.

"Good work, old horse," said this person. "Four left. Look--they're drawing off."

The white-robed horsemen were indeed reining away, clustering together just out of accurate rifle-range, as if in council. There had been seven when they had first swooped down on the comrades, but the fire from the two rifles in the sand-pit had been deadly.

"Look, sahib--they abandon the fray!"

Yar Ali stood up boldly and shouted taunts at the departing riders, one of whom whirled and sent a bullet that kicked up sand thirty feet in front of the pit.

"They shoot like the sons of dogs," said Yar Ali in complacent self-esteem. "By Allah, did you see that rogue plunge from his saddle as my lead went home? Up, sahib; let us run after them and cut them down!"

Paying no attention to this outrageous proposal-- for he knew it was but one of the gestures Afghan nature continually demands--Steve rose, dusted off his breeches and gazing after the riders, now white specks far out on the desert, said musingly: "Those fellows ride as if they had some set purpose in mind--not a bit like men running from a licking."

"Aye," agreed Yar Ali promptly and seeing nothing inconsistent with his present attitude and recent bloodthirsty suggestion, "they ride after more of their kind--they are hawks who give up their prey not quickly. We had best move our position quickly, Steve sahib. They will come back--maybe in a few hours, maybe in a few days--it all depends on how far away lies the oasis of their tribe. But they will be back. We have guns and lives--they want both. And behold."

The Afghan levered out the empty shell and slipped a single cartridge into the breech of his rifle.

"My last bullet, sahib."

Steve nodded. "I've got three left."

The raiders whom their bullets had knocked from the saddle had been looted by their own comrades. No use searching the bodies which lay in the sand for ammunition. Steve lifted his canteen and shook it. Not much water remained. He knew that Yar Ali had only a little more than he, though the big Afridi, bred in a barren land, had used and needed less water than did the American; although the latter, judged from a white man's standards, was hard and tough as a wolf. As Steve unscrewed the canteen cap and drank very sparingly, he mentally reviewed the chain of events that had led them to their present position.

Wanderers, soldiers of fortune, thrown together by chance and attracted to each other by mutual admiration, he and Yar Ali had wandered from India up through Turkistan and down through Persia, an oddly assorted but highly capable pair. Driven by the restless urge of inherent wanderlust, their avowed purpose--which they swore to and sometimes believed themselves--was the accumulation of some vague and undiscovered treasure, some pot of gold at the foot of some yet unborn rainbow.

Then in ancient Shiraz they had heard of the Fire of Asshurbanipal. From the lips of an ancient Persian trader, who only half believed what he repeated to them, they heard the tale that he in turn had heard from the babbling lips of delirium, in his distant youth. He had been a member of a caravan, fifty years before, which, wandering far on the southern shore of the Persian Gulf trading for pearls, had followed the tale of a rare pearl far into the desert.

The pearl, rumored found by a diver and stolen by a shaykh of the interior, they did not find, but they did pick up a Turk who was dying of starvation, thirst and a bullet wound in the thigh. As, he died in delirium, he babbled a wild tale of a silent dead city of black stone set in the drifting sands of the desert far to the westward, and of a flaming gem clutched in the bony fingers of a skeleton on an ancient throne.

He had not dared bring it away with him, because of an overpowering brooding horror that haunted the place, and thirst had driven him into the desert again, where Bedouins had pursued and wounded him. Yet he had escaped, riding hard until his horse fell under him. He died without telling how he had reached the mythical city in the first place, but the old trader thought he must have come from the northwest--a deserter from the Turkish army, making a desperate attempt to reach the Gulf.

The men of the caravan had made no attempt to plunge still further into the desert in search of the city; for, said the old trader, they believed it to be the ancient, ancient City of Evil spoken of in the Necronomicon of the mad Arab Alhazred--the city of the dead on which an ancient curse rested. Legends named it vaguely: the Arabs called it Beled-el-Djinn, the City of Devils, and the Turks, Karashehr, the Black City. And the gem was that ancient and accursed jewel belonging to a king of long ago, whom the Grecians called Sardanapalus and the Semitic peoples Asshurbanipal.

Steve had been fascinated by the tale. Admitting to himself that it was doubtless one of the ten thousand cock-and-bull myths booted about the East, still there was a possibility that he and Yar Ali had stumbled onto a trace of that pot of rainbow gold for which they searched. And Yar Ali had heard hints before of a silent city of the sands; tales had followed the eastbound caravans over the high Persian uplands and across the sands of Turkistan, into the mountain country and beyond--vague tales; whispers of a black city of the djinn, deep in the hazes of a haunted desert.

So, following the trail of the legend, the companions had come from Shiraz to a village on the Arabian shore of the Persian Gulf, and there had heard more from an old man who had been a pearl-diver in his youth. The loquacity of age was on him and he told tales repeated to him by wandering tribesmen who had them in turn from the wild nomads of the deep interior; and again Steve and Yar Ah heard of the still black city with giant beasts carved of stone, and the skeleton sultan who held the blazing gem.

And so, mentally swearing at himself for a fool, Steve had made the plunge, and Yar Ali, secure in the knowledge that all things lay on the lap of Allah, had come with him. Their scanty supply of money had been just sufficient to provide riding-camels and provisions for a bold flying invasion of the unknown. Their only chart had been the vague rumors that placed the supposed location of Kara-Shehr.

There had been days of hard travel, pushing the beasts and conserving water and food. Then, deep in the desert they invaded, they had encountered a blinding sand-wind in which they had lost the camels. After that came long miles of staggering through the sands, battered by a flaming sun, subsisting on rapidly dwindling water from their canteens, and food Yar Ali had in a pouch. No thought of finding the mythical city now. They pushed on blindly, in hope of stumbling upon a spring; they knew that behind them no oases lay within a distance they could hope to cover on foot. It was a desperate chance, but their only one.

Then white-clad hawks had swooped down on them, out of the haze of the skyline, and from a shallow and hastily scooped trench the adventurers had exchanged shots with the wild riders who circled them at top speed. The bullets of the Bedouins had skipped through their makeshift fortifications, knocking dust into their eyes and flicking bits of cloth from their garments, but by good chance neither had been hit.

Their one bit of luck, reflected Clarney, as he cursed himself for a fool. What a mad venture it had been, anyway! To think that two men could so dare the desert and live, much less wrest from its abysmal bosom the secrets of the ages! And that crazy tale of a skeleton hand gripping a flaming jewel in a dead city--bosh! What utter rot! He must have been crazy himself to credit it, the American decided with the clarity of view that suffering and danger bring.

"Well, old horse," said Steve, lifting his rifle, "let's get going. It's a toss-up if we die of thirst or get sniped off by the desert-brothers. Anyway, we're doin' no good here."

"God gives," agreed Yar Ali cheerfully. "The sun sinks westward. Soon the coolness of night will be upon us. Perhaps we shall find water yet, sahib. Look, the terrain changes to the south."

Clarney shaded his eyes against the dying sun. Beyond a level, barren expanse of several miles width, the land did indeed become more broken; aborted hills were in evidence. The American slung his rifle over his arm and sighed.

"Heave ahead; we're food for the buzzards anyhow."

The sun sank and the moon rose, flooding the desert with weird silver light. Drifted sand glimmered in long ripples, as if a sea had suddenly been frozen into immobility. Steve, parched fiercely by a thirst he dared not fully quench, cursed beneath his breath. The desert was beautiful beneath the moon, with the beauty of a cold marble lorelei to lure men to destruction. What a mad quest! his weary brain reiterated; the Fire of Asshurbanipal retreated into the mazes of unreality with each dragging step. The desert became not merely a material wasteland, but the gray mists of the lost eons, in whose depths dreamed sunken things.

Clarney stumbled and swore; was he failing already? Yar Ali swung along with the easy, tireless stride of the mountain man, and Steve set his teeth, nerving himself to greater effort. They were entering the broken country at last, and the going became harder. Shallow gullies and narrow ravines knifed the earth with wavering patterns. Most of them were nearly filled with sand, and there was no trace of water.

"This country was once oasis country," commented Yar Ali. "Allah knows how many centuries ago the sand took it, as the sand has taken so many cities in TurkiStan."

They swung on like dead men in a gray land of death.

The moon grew red and sinister as she sank, and shadowy darkness settled over the desert before they had reached a point where they could see what lay beyond the broken belt. Even the big Afghan's feet began to drag, and Steve kept himself erect only by a savage effort of will. At last they toiled up a sort of ridge, on the southern side of which the land sloped downward.

"We rest," declared Steve. "There's no water in this hellish country. No use in goin' on for ever. My legs are stiff as gun-barrels. I couldn't take another step to save my neck. Here's a kind of stunted cliff, about as high as a man's shoulder, facing south. We'll sleep in the lee of it."

"And shall we not keep watch, Steve sahib?"

"We don't," answered Steve. "If the Arabs cut our throats while we're asleep, so much the better. We're goners anyhow."

With which optimistic observation Clarney lay down stiffly in the deep sand. But Yar Ali stood, leaning forward, straining his eyes into the elusive darkness that turned the star-flecked horizons to murky wells of shadow.

"Something lies on the skyline to the south," he muttered uneasily. "A hill? I cannot tell, or even be sure that I see anything at all."

"You're seeing mirages already," said Steve irritably. "Lie down and sleep."

And so saying Steve slumbered.

The sun in his eyes awoke him. He sat up, yawning, and his first sensation was that of thirst. He lifted his canteen and wet his lips. One drink left. Yar Ali still slept. Steve's eyes wandered over the southern horizon and he started. He kicked the recumbent Afghan.

"Hey, wake up, Ali. I reckon you weren't seeing things after all. There's your hill--and a queer-lookin' one, too."

The Afridi woke as a wild thing wakes, instantly and completely, his hand leaping to his long knife as he glared about for enemies. His gaze followed Steve's pointing fingers and his eyes widened.

"By Allah and by Allah!" he swore. "We have come into a land of djinn! That is no hill--it is a city of stone in the midst of the sands!"

Steve bounded to his feet like a steel spring released. As he gazed with bated breath, a fierce shout escaped his lips. At his feet the slope of the ridge ran down into a wide and level expanse of sand that stretched away southward. And far away, across those sands, to his straining sight the 'hill' slowly took shape, like a mirage growing from the drifting sands.

He saw great uneven walls, massive battlements; all about crawled the sands like a living, sensate thing, drifted high about the walls, softening the rugged outlines. No wonder that at first glance the whole had appeared like a hill.

"Kara-Shehr!" Clarney exclaimed fiercely. "Beled-el-Djinn! The city of the dead! It wasn't a pipe-dream after all! We've found it--by Heaven, we've found it! Come on! Let's go!"

Yar Ali shook his head uncertainly and muttered something about evil djinn under his breath, but he followed. The sight of the ruins had swept from Steve his thirst and hunger, and the fatigue that a few hours' sleep had not fully overcome. He trudged on swiftly, oblivious to the rising heat, his eyes gleaming with the lust of the explorer. It was not altogether greed for the fabled gem that had prompted Steve Clarney to risk his life in that grim wilderness; deep in his soul lurked the age-old heritage of the white man, the urge to seek out the hidden places of the world, and that urge had been stirred to the depths by the ancient tales.

Now as they crossed the level wastes that separated the broken land from the city, they saw the shattered walls take clearer form and shape, as if they grew out of the morning sky. The city seemed built of huge blocks of black stone, but how high the walls had been there was no telling because of the sand that drifted high about their base; in many places they had fallen away and the sand hid the fragments entirely.

The sun reached her zenith and thirst intruded itself in spite of zeal and enthusiasm, but Steve fiercely mastered his suffering. His lips were parched and swollen, but he would not take that last drink until he had reached the ruined city. Yar Ali wet his lips from his own canteen and tried to share the remainder with his friend. Steve shook his head and plodded on.

In the ferocious heat of the desert afternoon they reached the ruin, and passing through a wide breach in the crumbling wall, gazed on the dead city. Sand choked the ancient streets and lent fantastic form to huge fallen and half-hidden columns. So crumbled into decay and so covered with sand was the whole that the explorers could make out little of the original plan of the city; now it was but a waste of drifted sand and crumbling stone over which brooded, like an invisible cloud, an aura of unspeakable antiquity.

But directly in front of them ran a broad avenue, the outline of which not even the ravaging sands and winds of time had been able to efface. On either side of the wide way were ranged huge columns, not unusually tall, even allowing for the sand that hid their bases, but incredibly massive. On the top of each column stood a figure carved from solid stone--great, somber images, half human, half bestial, partaking of the brooding brutishness of the whole city. Steve cried out in amazement.

"The winged bulls of Nineveh. The bulls with men's heads! By the saints, Ali, the old tales are true! The Assyrians did build this city! The whole tale's true! They must have come here when the Babylonians destroyed Assyriawhy, this scene's a dead ringer for pictures I've seen--reconstructed scenes of old Nineveh! And look!"

He pointed down the broad street to the great building which reared at the other end, a colossal, brooding edifice whose columns and walls of solid black stone blocks defied the winds and sands of time. The drifting, obliterating sea washed about its foundations, overflowing into its doorways, but it would require a thousand years to inundate the whole structure.

"An abode of devils!" muttered Yar Ali, uneasily.

"The temple of Baal!" exclaimed Steve. "Come on!--I was afraid we'd find all the palaces and temples hidden by the sand and have to dig for the gem."

"Little good it will do us," muttered Yar Ali. "Here we die."

"I reckon so." Steve unscrewed the cap of his canteen. "Let's take our last drink. Anyway, we're safe from the Arabs. They'd never dare come here, with their superstitions. We'll drink and then we'll die, I reckon, but first we'll find the jewel. When I pass out, I want to have it in my hand. Maybe a few centuries later some lucky son-of-a-gun will find our skeletons--and the gem. Here's to him, whoever he is!"

With which grim jest Clarney drained his canteen and Yar Ali followed suit. They had played their last ace; the rest lay on the lap of Allah.

They strode up the broad way, and Yar Ali, utterly fearless in the face of human foci, glanced nervously to tight and left, half expecting to see a horned and fantastic face leering at him from behind a column. Steve felt the somber antiquity of the place, and almost found himself fearing a rush of bronze war chariots down the forgotten streets, or to hear the sudden menacing flare of bronze trumpets. The silence in dead cities was so much more intense, he reflected, than that on the open desert.

They came to the portals of the great temple. Rows of immense columns flanked the wide doorway, which was ankle-deep in sand, and from which sagged massive bronze frameworks that had once braced mighty doors, whose polished woodwork had rotted away centuries ago. They passed into a mighty hall of misty twilight whose shadowy stone roof was upheld by columns like the trunks of forest trees. The whole effect of the architecture was one of awesome magnitude and sullen, breathtaking splendor, like a temple built by somber giants for the abode of dark gods.

Yar--Ali walked fearfully, as if he expected to awake sleeping gods, and Steve, without the Afridi's superstitions, yet felt the gloomy majesty of the place lay somber hands on his soul.

No trace of a footprint showed in the deep dust on the floor; half a century had passed since the affrighted and devilridden Turk had fled these silent halls. As for the Bedouins, it was easy to see why those superstitious sons of the desert shunned this haunted city--and haunted it was, not by actual ghosts, perhaps, but by the shadows of lost splendors.

As they trod the sands of the hall, which seemed endless, Steve pondered many questions: How did these fugitives from the wrath of frenzied rebels build this city? How did they pass through the country of their foes--for Babylonia lay between Assyria and the Arabian desert. Yet there had been no other place for them to go; westward lay Syria and the sea, and north and east swarmed the 'dangerous Medes', those fierce Aryans whose aid had stiffened the arm of Babylon to smite her foe to the dust.

Possibly, thought Steve, Kara-Shehr--whatever its name had been in those dim days--had been built as an outpost border city before the fall of the Assyrian empire, whither survivals of that overthrow fled. At any rate it was possible that Kara-Shehr had outlasted Nineveh by some centuries--a strange, hermit city, no doubt, cut off from the rest of the world.

Surely, as Yar Ali had said, this was once fertile country, watered by oases; and doubtless in the broken country they had passed over the night before, there had been quarries that furnished the stone for the building of the city.

Then what caused its downfall? Did the encroachment of the sands and the filling up of the springs cause the people to abandon it, or was Kara-Shehr a city of silence before the sands crept over the walls? Did the downfall come from within or without? Did civil war blot out the inhabitants, or were they slaughtered by some powerful foe from the desert? Clarney shook his head in baffled chagrin. The answers to those questions were lost in the maze of forgotten ages.

"Allaho akbar!" They had traversed the great shadowy hall and at its further end they came upon a hideous black stone altar, behind which loomed an ancient god, bestial and horrific. Steve shrugged his shoulders as he recognized the monstrous aspect of the image--aye, that was Baal, on which black altar in other ages many a screaming, writhing, naked victim had offered up its naked soul. The idol embodied in its utter, abysmal and sullen bestiality the whole soul of this demoniac city. Surely, thought Steve, the builders of Nineveh and Kara-Shehr were cast in another mold from the people of today. Their art and culture were too ponderous, too grimly barren of the lighter aspects of humanity, to be wholly human, as modern man understands humanity.

Their architecture was repellent; of high skill, yet so massive, sullen and brutish in effect as to be almost beyond the comprehension of moderns.

The adventurers passed through a narrow door which opened in the end of the hall close to the idol, and came into a series of wide, dim, dusty chambers connected by column-flanked corridors. Along these they strode in the gray ghostly light, and came at last to a wide stair, whose massive stone steps led upward and vanished in the gloom. Here Yar Ali halted.

"We have dared much, sahib," he muttered. "Is it wise to dare more?"

Steve, aquiver with eagerness, yet understood the Afghan's mind. "You mean we shouldn't go up those stairs?"

"They have an evil look. To what chambers of silence and horror may they lead? When djinn haunt deserted buildings, they lurk in the upper chambers. At any moment a demon may bite off our heads."

"We're dead men anyhow," grunted Steve. "But I tell you--you go on back through the hall and watch for the Arabs while I go upstairs."

"Watch for a wind on the horizon," responded the Afghan gloomily, shifting his rifle and loosening his long knife in its scabbard. "No Bedouin comes here. Lead on, sahib. Thou'rt mad after the manner of all Franks,--but I would not leave thee to face the djinn alone."

So the companions mounted the massive stairs, their feet sinking deep into the accumulated dust of centuries at each step. Up and up they went, to an incredible height until the depths below merged into a vague gloom.

"We walk blind to our doom, sahib," muttered Yar Ali. "Allah il allah--and Muhammad is his Prophet! Nevertheless, I feel the presence of slumbering Evil and never again shall I hear the wind blowing up the Khyber Pass."

Steve made no reply. He did not like the breathless silence that brooded over the ancient temple, nor the grisly gray light that filtered from some hidden source.

Now above them the gloom lightened somewhat and they emerged into a vast circular chamber, grayly illumined by light that filtered in through the high, pierced ceiling. But another radiance lent itself to the illumination. A cry burst from Steve's lips, echoed by Yar Ali.

Standing on the top step of the broad stone stair, they looked directly across the broad chamber, with its dustcovered heavy tile floor and bare black stone walls. From about the center of the chamber, massive steps led up to a stone dais, and on this dais stood a marble throne. About this throne glowed and shimmered an uncanny light, and the awestruck adventurers gasped as they saw its source. On the throne slumped a human skeleton, an almost shapeless mass of moldering bones. A fleshless hand sagged outstretched upon the broad marble throne-arm, and in its grisly clasp there pulsed and throbbed like a living thing, a great crimson stone.

The Fire of Asshurbanipal! Even after they had found the lost city Steve had not really allowed himself to believe that they would find the gem, or that it even existed in reality. Yet he could not doubt the evidence of his eyes, dazzled by that evil, incredible glow. With a fierce shout he sprang across the chamber and up the steps. Yar Ali was at his heels, but when Steve would have seized the gem, the Afghan laid a hand on his arm.

"Wait!" exclaimed the big Muhammadan. "Touch it not yet, sahib! A curse lies on ancient things--and surely this is a thing triply accursed! Else why has it lain here untouched in a country of thieves for so many centuries? It is not well to disturb the possessions of the dead."

"Bosh!" snorted the American. "Superstitions! The Bedouins were scared by the tales that have come down to 'em from their ancestors. Being desert-dwellers they mistrust cities anyway, and no doubt this one had an evil reputation in its lifetime. And nobody except Bedouins have seen this place before, except that Turk, who was probably half demented with suffering.

"These bones may be those of the king mentioned in the legend--the dry desert air preserves such things indefinitely-

-but I doubt it. Maybe Assyrian--most likely Arab--some beggar that got the gem and then died on that throne for some reason or other."

The Afghan scarcely heard him. He was gazing in fearful fascination at the great stone, as a hypnotized bird stares into a serpent's eye.

"Look at it, sahib!" he whispered. "What is it? No such gem as this was ever cut by mortal hands! Look how it throbs and pulses like the heart of a cobra!"

Steve was looking, and he was aware of a strange undefined feeling of uneasiness. Well versed in the knowledge of precious stones, he had never seen a stone like this. At first glance he had supposed it to be a monster ruby, as told in the legends. Now he was not sure, and he had a nervous feeling that Yar Ali was right, that this was no natural, normal gem: He could not classify the style in which it was cut, and such was the power of its lurid radiance that he found it difficult to gaze at it closely for any length of time. The whole setting was not one calculated to soothe restless nerves. The deep dust on the floor suggested an unwholesome antiquity; the gray light evoked a sense of unreality, and the heavy black walls towered grimly, hinting at hidden things.

"Let's take the stone, and go!" muttered Steve, an unaccustomed panicky dread rising in his bosom.

"Wait!" Yar Ali's eyes were blazing, and he gazed, not at the gem, but at the sullen stone walls. "We are flies in the lair of the spider! Sahib, as Allah lives, it is more than the ghosts of old fears that lurk over this city of horror! I feel the presence of peril, as I have felt it before--as I felt it in a jungle cavern where a python lurked unseen in the darkness--as I felt it in the temple of Thuggee where the hidden stranglers of Siva crouched to spring upon us--as I feel it now, tenfold!"

Steve's hair prickled. He knew that Yar Ali was a grim veteran, not to be stampeded by silly fear or senseless panic; he well remembered the incidents referred to by the Afghan, as he remembered other occasions upon which Yar Ali's Oriental telepathic instinct had warned him of danger before that danger was seen or heard.

"What is it, Yar Ali?" he whispered.

The Afghan shook his head, his eyes filled with a weird mysterious light as he listened to the dim occult promptings of his subconsciousness.

"I know not; I know it is close to us, and that it is very ancient and very evil. I think--" Suddenly he halted and wheeled, the eery light vanishing from his eyes to be replaced by a glare of wolf-like fear and suspicion.

"Hark, sahib!" he snapped. "Ghosts or dead men mount the stair!"

Steve stiffened as the stealthy pad of soft sandals on stone reached his ear.

"By Judas, Ali!" he rapped; "something's out there--"

The ancient walls re-echoed to a chorus of wild yells as a horde of savage figures flooded the chamber. For one dazed insane instant Steve believed wildly that they were being attacked by re-embodied warriors of a vanished age; then the spiteful crack of a bullet past his ear and the acrid smell of powder told him that their foes were material enough. Clarney cursed; in their fancied security--they had been caught like rats in a trap by the pursuing Arabs.

Even as the American threw up his rifle, Yar Ali fired point-blank from the hip with deadly effect, hurled his empty rifle into the horde and went down the steps like a hurricane, his three-foot Khyber knife shimmering in his hairy hand. Into his gusto for battle went real relief that his foes were human. A bullet ripped the turban from his head, but an Arab went down with a split skull beneath the hillman's first, shearing stroke.

A tall Bedouin clapped his gun-muzzle to the Afghan's side, but before he could pull the trigger, Clarney's bullet scattered his brains. The very number of the attackers hindered their onslaught on the big Afridi, whose tigerish quickness made shooting as dangerous to themselves as to him. The bulk of them swarmed about him, striking with scimitar and rifle-stock while others charged up the steps after Steve. At that range there was no missing; the American simply thrust his rifle muzzle into a bearded face and blasted it into a ghastly ruin. The others came on, screaming like panthers.

And now as he prepared to expend his last cartridge, Clarney saw two things in one flashing instant--a wild warrior who, with froth on his beard and a heavy scimitar uplifted, was almost upon him, and another who knelt on the floor drawing a careful bead on the plunging Yar Ali. Steve made an instant choice and fired over the shoulder of the charging swordsman, killing the rifleman--and voluntarily offering his own life for his friend's; for the scimitar was swinging at his own head. But even as the Arab swung, grunting with the force of the blow, his sandaled foot slipped on the marble steps and the curved blade, veering erratically from its arc, clashed on Steve's rifle-barrel. In an instant the American clubbed his rifle, and as the Bedouin recovered his balance and again heaved up the scimitar, Clarney struck with all his rangy power, and stock and skull shattered together.

Then a heavy ball smacked into his shoulder, sickening him with the shock.

As he staggered dizzily, a Bedouin whipped a turbancloth about his feet and jerked viciously. Clarney pitched headlong down the steps, to strike with stunning force. A gun-stock in a brown hand went up to dash out his brains, but an imperious command halted the blow.

"Slay him not, but bind him hand and foot."

As Steve struggled dazedly against many gripping hands, it seemed to him that somewhere he had heard that imperious voice before.

The American's downfall had occurred in a matter of seconds. Even as Steve's second shot had cracked, Yar Ali had half severed a raider's arm and himself received a numbing blow from a rifle-stock on his left shoulder. His sheepskin coat, worn despite the desert heat, saved his hide from half a dozen slashing knives. A rifle was discharged so close to his face that the powder burnt him fiercely, bringing a bloodthirsty yell from the maddened Afghan. As Yar Ali swung up his dripping blade the rifleman, ashy-faced, lifted his rifle above his head in both hands to parry the downward blow, whereat the Afridi, with a yelp of ferocious exultation, shifted as a junglecat strikes and plunged his long knife into the Arab's belly. But at that instant a rifle-stock, swung with all the hearty ill-will its wielder could evoke, crashed against the giant's head, laying open the scalp and dashing him to his knees.

With the dogged and silent ferocity of his breed, Yar Ali staggered blindly up again, slashing at foes he could scarcely see, but a storm of blows battered him down again, nor did his attackers cease beating him until he lay still. They would have finished him in short order then, but for another peremptory order from their chief; whereupon they bound the senseless knife-man and flung him down alongside Steve, who was fully conscious and aware of the savage hurt of the bullet in his shoulder.

He glared up at the tall Arab who stood looking down at him.

"Well, sahib," said this one--and Steve saw he was no Bedouin--"do you not remember me?"

Steve scowled; a bullet-wound is no aid to concentration.

"You look familiar--by Judas!--you are! Nureddin El Mekru!"

"I am honored! The sahib remembers!" Nureddin salaamed mockingly. "And you remember, no doubt, the occasion on which you made me a present of--this!"

The dark eyes shadowed with bitter menace and the shaykh indicated a thin white scar on the angle of his jaw.

"I remember," snarled Clarney, whom pain and anger did not tend to make docile. "It was in Somaliland, years ago. You were in the slave-trade then. A wretch of a nigger escaped from you and took refuge with me. You walked into my camp one night in your high-handed way, started a row and in the ensuing scrap you got a butcher-knife across your face. I wish I'd cut your lousy throat."

"You had your chance," answered the Arab. "Now the tables are turned."

"I thought your stamping-ground lay west," growled Clarney; "Yemen and the Somali country."

"I quit the slave-trade long ago," answered the shaykh. "It is an outworn game. I led a band of thieves in Yemen for a time; then again I was forced to change my location. I came here with a few faithful followers, and by Allah, those wild men nearly slit my throat at first. But I overcame their suspicions, and now I lead more men than have followed me in years.

"They whom you fought off yesterday were my men-- scouts I had sent out ahead. My oasis lies far to the west. We have ridden for many days, for I was on my way to this very city. When my scouts rode in and told me of two wanderers, I did not alter my course, for I had business first in Beled-el-Djinn. We rode into the city from the west and saw your tracks in the sand. We followed there, and you were blind buffalo who heard not our coming."

Steve snarled. "You wouldn't have caught us so easy, only we thought no Bedouin would dare come into Kara-Shehr."

Nureddin nodded. "But I am no Bedouin. I have traveled far and seen many lands and many races, and I have read many books. I know that fear is smoke, that the dead are dead, and that djinn and ghosts and curses are mists that the wind blows away. It was because of the tales of the red stone that I came into this forsaken desert. But it has taken months to persuade my men to ride with me here.

"But--I am here! And your presence is a delightful surprize. Doubtless you have guessed why I had you taken alive; I have more elaborate entertainment planned for you and that Pathan swine. Now--I take the Fire of Asshurbanipal and we will go."

He turned toward the dais, and one of his men, a bearded one-eyed giant, exclaimed, "Hold, my lord! Ancient evil reigned here before. the days of Muhammad! The djinn howl through these halls when the winds blow, and men have seen ghosts dancing on the walls beneath the moon. No man of mortals has dared this black city for a thousand years--save one, half a century ago, who fled shrieking.

"You have come here from Yemen; you do not know the ancient curse on this foul city, and this evil stone, which pulses like the red heart of Satan! We have followed you here against our judgment, because you have proven yourself a strong man, and have said you hold a charm against all evil beings. You said you but wished to look on this mysterious gem, but now we see it is your intention to take it for yourself. Do not offend the djinn!"

"Nay, Nureddin, do not offend the djinn!" chorused the other Bedouins. The shaykh's own hard-bitten ruffians, standing in a compact group somewhat apart from the Bedouins, said nothing; hardened to crimes and deeds of impiety, they were less affected by the superstitions of the desert men, to whom the dread tale of the accursed city had been repeated for centuries. Steve, even while hating Nureddin with concentrated venom, realized the magnetic power of the man, the innate leadership that had enabled him to overcome thus far the fears and traditions of ages.

"The curse is laid on infidels who invade the city," answered Nureddin, "not on the Faithful. See, in this chamber have we overcome our kafar foes!"

A white-bearded desert hawk shook his head.

"The curse is more ancient than Muhammad, and recks not of race or creed. Evil men reared this black city in the dawn of the Beginnings of Days. They oppressed our ancestors of the black tents, and warred among themselves; aye, the black walls of this foul city were stained with blood, and echoed to the shouts of unholy revel and the whispers of dark intrigues.

"Thus came the stone to the city: there dwelt a magician at the court of Asshurbanipal, and the black wisdom of ages was not denied to him. To gain honor and power for himself, he dared the horrors of a nameless vast cavern in a dark, untraveled land, and from those fiendhaunted depths he brought that blazing gem, which is carved of the frozen flames of Hell! By reason of his fearful power in black magic, he put a spell on the demon which guarded the ancient gem, and so stole away the stone. And the demon slept in the cavern unknowing.

"So this magician--Xuthltan by name--dwelt in the court of the sultan Asshurbanipal and did magic and forecast events by scanning the lurid deeps of the stone, into which no eyes but his could look unblinded. And men called the stone the Fire of Asshurbanipal, in honor of the king.

"But evil came upon the kingdom and men cried out that it was the curse of the djinn, and the sultan in great fear bade Xuthltan take the gem and cast it into the cavern from which he had taken it, lest worse ill befall them.

"Yet it was not the magician's will to give up the gem wherein he read strange secrets of pre-Adamite days, and he fled to the rebel city of Kara-Shehr, where soon civil war broke out and men strove with one another to possess the gem. Then the king who ruled the city, coveting the stone, seized the magician and put him to death by torture, and in this very room he watched him die; with the gem in his hand the king sat upon the throne--even as he has sat upon the throne--even as he has sat throughout the centuries--even as now he sits!"

The Arab's finger stabbed at the moldering bones on the marble throne, and the wild desert men blenched; even Nureddin's own scoundrels recoiled, catching their breath, but the shaykh showed no sign of perturbation.

"As Xuthltan died," continued the old Bedouin, "he cursed the stone whose magic had not saved him, and he shrieked aloud the fearful words which undid the spell he had put upon the demon in the cavern, and set the monster free. And crying out on the forgotten gods, Cthulhu and Koth and Yog-Sothoth, and all the pre-Adamite Dwellers in the black cities under the sea and the caverns of the earth, he called upon them--to take back that which was theirs, and with his dying breath pronounced doom on the false king, and that doom was that the king should sit on his throne holding in his hand the Fire of Asshurbanipal until the thunder of Judgment Day.

"Thereat the great stone cried out as a live thing cries, and the king and his soldiers saw a black cloud spinning up from the floor, and out of the cloud blew a fetid wind, and out of the wind came a grisly shape which stretched forth fearsome paws and laid them on the king, who shriveled and died at their touch. And the soldiers fled screaming, and all the people of the city ran forth wailing into the desert, where they perished or gained through the wastes to the far oasis towns. Kara-Shehr lay silent and deserted, the haunt of the lizard and the jackal. And when some of the desert people ventured into the city they found the king dead on his throne, clutching the blazing gem, but they dared not lay hand upon it, for they knew the demon lurked near to guard it through all the ages as he lurks near even as we stand here."

The warriors shuddered involuntarily and glanced about, and Nureddin said, "Why did he not come forth when the Franks entered the chamber? Is he deaf, that the sound of the combat has not awakened him?"

"We have not touched the gem," answered the old Bedouin, "nor had the Franks molested it. Men have looked on it and lived; but no mortal may touch it and survive."

Nureddin started to speak, gazed at the stubborn, uneasy faces and realized the futility of argument. His attitude changed abruptly.

"I am master here," he snapped, dropping a hand to his holster. "I have not sweat and bled for this gem to be balked at the last by groundless fears! Stand back, all! Let any man cross me at the peril of his head!"

He faced them, his eyes blazing, and they fell back, cowed by the force of his ruthless personality. He strode boldly up the marble steps, and the Arabs caught their breath, recoiling toward the door; Yar Ali, conscious at last, groaned dismally. God! thought Steve, what a barbaric scene!--bound captives on the dust-heaped floor, wild warriors clustered about, gripping their weapons, the raw acrid scent of blood and burnt powder still fouling the air, corpses strewn in a horrid welter of blood, brains and entrails--and on the dais, the hawk-faced shaykh, oblivious to all except the evil crimson glow in the skeleton fingers that rested on the marble throne.

A tense silence gripped all as Nureddin stretched forth his hand slowly, as if hypnotized by the throbbing crimson light. And in Steve's subconsciousness there shuddered a dim echo, as of something vast and loathsome waking suddenly from an age-long slumber. The American's eyes moved instinctively toward the grim cyclopean walls. The jewel's glow had altered strangely; it burned a deeper, darker red, angry and menacing.

"Heart of all evil," murmured the shaykh, "how many princes died for thee in the Beginnings of Happenings? Surely the blood of kings throbs in thee. The sultans and the princesses and the generals who wore thee, they are dust and are forgotten, but thou blazest with majesty undimmed, fire of the world--"

Nureddin seized the stone. A shuddery wail broke from the Arabs, cut through by a sharp inhuman cry. To Steve it seemed, horribly, that the great jewel had cried out like a living thing! The stone slipped from the shaykh's hand. Nureddin might have dropped it; to Steve it looked as though it leaped convulsively, as a live thing might leap. It rolled from the dais, bounding from step to step, with Nureddin springing after it, cursing as his clutching hand missed it. It struck the floor, veered sharply, and despite the deep dust, rolled like a revolving ball of fire toward the back wall. Nureddin was close upon it--it struck the wall--the shaykh's hand reached for it.

A scream of mortal fear ripped the tense silence. Without warning the solid wall had opened. Out of the black wall that gaped there, a tentacle shot and gripped the shaykh's body as a python girdles its victim, and jerked him headlong into the darkness. And then the wall showed blank and solid once more; only from within sounded a hideous, high-pitched, muffled screaming that chilled the blood of the listeners. Howling wordlessly, the Arabs stampeded, jammed in a battling, screeching mass in the doorway, tore through and raced madly down the wide stairs.

Steve and Yar Ali, lying helplessly, heard the frenzied clamor of their flight fade away into the distance, and gazed in dumb horror at the grim wall. The shrieks had faded into a more horrific silence. Holding their breath, they heard suddenly a sound that froze the blood in their veins- -the soft sliding of metal or stone in a groove. At the same time the hidden door began to open, and Steve caught a glimmer in the blackness that might have been the glitter of monstrous eyes. He closed his own eyes; he dared not look upon whatever horror slunk from that hideous black well. He knew that there are strains the human brain cannot stand, and every primitive instinct in his soul cried out to him that this thing was nightmare and lunacy. He sensed that Yar Ali likewise closed his eyes, and the two lay like dead men.

Clarney heard no sound, but he sensed the presence of a horrific evil too grisly for human comprehension--of an Invader from Outer Gulfs and far black reaches of cosmic being. A deadly cold pervaded the chamber, and Steve felt the glare of inhuman eyes sear through his closed lids and freeze his consciousness. If he looked, if he opened his eyes, he knew stark black madness would be his instant lot.

He felt a soul-shakingly foul breath against his face and knew that the monster was bending close above him, but he lay like a man frozen in a nightmare. He clung to one thought: neither he nor Yar Ali had touched the jewel this horror guarded.

Then he no longer smelled the foul odor, the coldness in the air grew appreciably less, and he heard again the secret door slide in its groove. The fiend was returning to its hiding-place. Not all the legions of Hell could have prevented Steve's eyes from opening a trifle. He had only a glimpse as the hidden door slid to--and that one glimpse was enough to drive all consciousness from his brain. Steve Clarney, iron-nerved adventurer, fainted for the only time in his checkered life.

How long he lay there Steve never knew, but it could not have been long, for he was roused by Yar Ali's whisper, "Lie still, sahib, a little shifting of my body and I can reach thy cords with my teeth."

Steve felt the Afghan's powerful teeth at work on his bonds, and as he lay with his face jammed into the thick dust, and his wounded shoulder began to throb agonizingly--he had forgotten it until now--he began to gather the wandering threads of his consciousness, and it all came back to him. How much, he wondered dazedly, had been the nightmares of delirium, born from suffering and the thirst that caked his throat? The fight with the Arabs had been real--the bonds and the wounds showed that--but the grisly doom of the shaykh--the thing that had crept out of the black entrance in the wall--surely that had been a figment of delirium. Nureddin had fallen into a well or pit of some sort--Stave felt his hands were free and he rose to a sitting posture, fumbling for a pocket-knife the Arabs had overlooked. He did not look up or about the chamber as he slashed the cords that bound his ankles, and then freed Yar Ali, working awkwardly because his left arm was stiff and useless.

"Where are the Bedouins?" he asked, as the Afghan rose, lifting him to his feet.

"Allah, sahib," whispered Yar Ali, "are you mad? Have you forgotten? Let us go quickly before the djinn returns!"

"It was a nightmare," muttered Steve. "Look--the jewel is back on the throne--" His voice died out. Again that red glow throbbed about the ancient throne, reflecting from the moldering skull; again in the outstretched finger-bones pulsed the Fire of Asshurbanipal. But at the foot of the throne lay another object that had not been there before--the severed head of Nureddin el Mekru stared sightlessly up at the gray light filtering through the stone ceiling. The bloodless lips were drawn back from the teeth in a ghastly grin, the staring eyes mirrored an intolerable horror. In the thick dust of the floor three spoors showed--one of the shaykh's where he had followed the red jewel as it rolled to the wall, and above it two other sets of tracks, coming to the throne and returning to the wall--vast, shapeless tracks, as of splayed feet, taloned and gigantic, neither human nor animal.

"My God!" choked Steve. "It was true--and the Thing--the Thing I saw--"

Steve remembered the flight from that chamber as a rushing nightmare, in which he and his companion hurtled headlong down an endless stair that was a gray well of fear, raced blindly through dusty silent chambers, past the glowering idol in the mighty hall and into the blazing light of the desert sun, where they fell slavering, fighting for breath.

Again Steve was roused by the Afridi's voice: "Sahib, sahib, in the Name of Allah the Compassionate, our luck has turned!"

Steve looked at his companion as a man might look in a trance: The big Afghan's garments were in tatters, and blood-soaked. He was stained with dust and caked with blood, and his voice was a croak. But his eyes were alight with hope and he pointed with a trembling finger.

"In the shade of yon ruined wall!" he croaked, striving to moisten his blackened lips. "Allah il allah! The horses of the men we killed! With canteens and food-pouches at the saddle-horns! Those dogs fled without halting for the steeds of their comrades!"

New life surged up into Steve's bosom and he rose, staggering.

"Out of here," he mumbled. "Out of here, quick!"

Like dying men they stumbled to the horses, tore them loose and climbed fumblingly into the saddles.

"We'll lead the spare mounts," croaked Steve, and Yar Ali nodded emphatic agreement.

"Belike we shall need them ere we sight the coast."

Though their tortured nerves screamed for the water that swung in canteens at the saddle-horns, they turned the mounts aside and, swaying in the saddle, rode like flying corpses down the long sandy street of Kara-Shehr, between the ruined palaces and the crumbling columns, crossed the fallen wall and swept out into the desert. Not once did either glance back toward that black pile of ancient horror, nor did either speak until the ruins faded into the hazy distance. Then and only then did they draw rein and ease their thirst.

"Allah il allah!" said Yar Ali piously. "Those dogs have beaten me until it is as though every bone in my body were broken. Dismount, I beg thee, sahib, and let me probe for that accursed bullet, and dress thy shoulder to the best of my meager ability."

While this was going on, Yar Ali spoke, avoiding his friend's eye, "You said, sahib, you said something about--about seeing? What saw ye, in Allah's name?"

A strong shudder shook the American's steely fray "You didn't look when--when the--the Thing put back the jewel in the skeleton's hand and left Nureddin's head on the dais?"

"By Allah, not I!" swore Yar Ali. "My eyes were as closed as if they had been welded together by the molten irons of Satan!"

Steve made no reply until the comrades had once more swung into the saddle and started on their long trek for the coast, which, with spare horses, food, water and weapons, they had a good chance to reach.

"I looked," the American said somberly. "I wish I had not; I know I'll dream about it for the rest of my life. I had only a glance; I couldn't describe it as a man describes an earthly thing. God help me, it wasn't earthly or sane either. Mankind isn't the first owner of the earth; there were Beings here before his coming--and now, survivals of hideously ancient epochs. Maybe spheres of alien dimensions press unseen on this material universe today. Sorcerers have called up sleeping devils before now and controlled them with magic. It is not unreasonable to suppose an Assyrian magician could invoke an elemental demon out of the earth to avenge him and guard something that must have come out of Hell in the first place."

"I'll try to tell you what I glimpsed; then we'll never speak of it again. It was gigantic and black and shadowy; it was a hulking monstrosity that walked upright like a man, but it was like a toad, too, and it was winged and tentacled. I saw only its back; if I'd seen the front of it--its face--I'd have undoubtedly lost my mind. The old Arab was right; God help us, it was the monster that Xuthltan called up out of the dark blind caverns of the earth to guard the Fire of Asshurbanipal!"

THE END

www.ingramcontent.com/pod-product-compliance
Lightning Source LLC
Chambersburg PA
CBHW030241180626
46810CB00008B/3234